SUPER MONSTERS™

SUN DOWN, MONSTERS UP!

Adapted by Meredith Rusu

Copyright © 2019 Netflix
Netflix Official Merchandise

ISBN 978-1-338-35493-5

10 9 8 7 6 5 4 3 2 1   19 20 21 22 23

Printed in the U.S.A.   40
First printing 2019

Book design by Jessica Meltzer

SCHOLASTIC INC.

Welcome to Pitchfork Pines Preschool, a super-cool school with some super-special students. Here, the fun starts when the sun goes down because the students are all children of famous monsters!

Every evening, Drac, Katya, Frankie, Lobo, and Cleo arrive looking like normal preschoolers. But the moment the sun sets, they transform into Super Monsters with special powers.

3

LOBO is a werewolf who can run super-fast.

KATYA is a witch who can cast spells with a wave of her crystal wand.

DRAC is a vampire. He can fly and loves impressing his friends.

FRANKIE is a kid-sized Frankenstein's monster with incredible strength.

And **CLEO** is a mummy princess who can control elements like wind and water.

But don't be frightened. These monsters aren't scary. They're actually really friendly! They all want to grow up to be the best monsters they can be, just like their parents.

One evening, right before sunset, the Super Monsters arrived at school.

"Did you hear?" Katya asked her friends. "There's a new girl starting school today!"

Sure enough, their teachers,
Igor and Esmie, brought a little girl they
had never seen before into the classroom.

"Everyone, this is Zoe," Igor said.

"Hi, Zoe!" cried all the Super Monsters.

"Hello," Zoe replied quietly. She was a little shy.

"You're just in time for our favorite part of the day," Esmie told Zoe. "The sun is about to set."

The friends all raced to the window. "Sun down. Monsters up!"

In a bright flash, Drac, Katya, Frankie, Lobo, and Cleo transformed into Super Monsters!

Everyone turned to Zoe. They were all curious about what type of monster she would be.

Zoe curtsied . . . and transformed into a zombie with bright blue skin and rainbow-colored hair!

"Wow!" cried Frankie. "You're a zombie!"

"That is so cool!" said Drac.

"Thanks," Zoe giggled. But she still seemed a little shy.

Pretty soon it was playtime. Everyone ran into the backyard. They were excited to play hide-and-go-shriek under the full moon.

Everyone, that is, except for Zoe. She sat by herself against the playground wall.

"Don't you want to play with your new friends?" Igor asked her.

"They seem nice," Zoe said quietly. "But it's all so different."

Igor nodded. "I understand. It can be hard getting used to new places."

"Maybe if you did something familiar, you'd feel better," Esmie told her. "What's something you like to do?"

"I like to paint," Zoe said.

Esmie winked and pulled out a big basket of colorful paints and brushes. "That sounds like a great idea."

Just then, Drac swooped down in a big loop.

"You're a really good flier," Zoe told him.

"Thanks!" said Drac. "But on my first day of preschool, I was so nervous, I flew into a tree!"

"Really?" Zoe giggled.

Katya waved her wand. "And I was so scared, I turned myself into a frog."

"But now we know preschool is totally awesome!" Lobo called while sprinting past.

"It helps us learn to control our monster powers," Frankie said.

"So we can grow up to be the best Super Monsters we can be," Cleo finished.

"Speaking of the best." Lobo crept up beside Cleo.
"I'm the best at playing monster tag. And . . . tag!
You're it!" Lobo tagged Cleo and dashed off.

"Hey! No fair!" yelled Cleo. "I wasn't ready!"

"Wait for us!" shouted Drac, Katya, and Frankie.

Zoe watched as the others all ran off to play monster tag. They were all so friendly. She was starting to feel a lot less nervous. In fact, she was starting to have an idea.

A little while later, the Super Monsters were busy using their powers to win the game of tag.

"I'm going to catch you!" Lobo zipped in and out between the bushes.

"You can't reach me up here!" Drac yelled from the sky.
Cleo sent a gust of wind his way. "That's what you think!"
With all the swooping and zooming and whooshing, it wasn't
long before everyone toppled over in a big pile on the ground!

The friends laughed and laughed when, suddenly, they heard a voice.
"You guys all look so silly!"
"Huh?" asked Frankie. "That sounded like Zoe. Where is she?"
They looked around, but Zoe wasn't anywhere in sight.

"I'm right here!" Zoe called. Then she walked through the playground wall!

"Wow!" They gasped. "Your monster power is walking through walls!"

"Yes!" Zoe smiled. "I can see through them too. That's how I saw you! And I have something to show you. Come and see!"

The friends followed her around the wall . . . and discovered
that Zoe had painted a beautiful picture of them!

"You did this?" Drac asked, amazed.

"Zoe, it's beautiful!" exclaimed Cleo.

"Thanks, everybody!" Zoe beamed. "I was nervous when I got here. But you're all so nice, and I had so much fun. I really like it here!"

Just then, the sky grew brighter. It was morning.

"Sun up!" the friends cried. In a flash, they transformed back into human mode. It was time to go home.

It had been an awesome night at Pitchfork Pines Preschool. And the Super Monsters couldn't wait to come back and have even more fun the next night. Because as long as they were together, there were sure to be more monster-sized adventures in store!